THE BANK
OF RANGOON

THE BANK OF RANGOON

R. O. Willis

THE BANK OF RANGOON

This is a work of fiction. All of the characters, names, incidents, organizations, and dialogue in this novel are either the products of the author's imagination or are used fictitiously.

iUniverse books may be ordered through booksellers or by contacting:

iUniverse
1663 Liberty Drive
Bloomington, IN 47403
www.iuniverse.com
1-800-Authors (1-800-288-4677)

Because of the dynamic nature of the Internet, any web addresses or links contained in this book may have changed since publication and may no longer be valid. The views expressed in this work are solely those of the author and do not necessarily reflect the views of the publisher, and the publisher hereby disclaims any responsibility for them.

Any people depicted in stock imagery provided by Thinkstock are models, and such images are being used for illustrative purposes only.
Certain stock imagery © Thinkstock.

ISBN: 978-1-5320-0567-1 (sc)
ISBN: 978-1-5320-0564-0 (e)

Library of Congress Control Number: 2016914518

Print information available on the last page.

iUniverse rev. date: 09/10/2016

INTRODUCTION

RANGOON WAS THE pearl of Burma from 1939 to March 1942. It was where some of the best food and wine could be found along with first-class hotels and casinos anywhere in the Indies. It was where generals and diplomats from both sides of the fence rubbed shoulders with businessmen from Europe and the United States and the greatest and richest smugglers in China.

Some there would cut your throat to get your gold teeth if you had any.

Whatever you desired—including pearls, jade, ivory, gold, or pretty bodies—could be found in Rangoon. Tourists crowded shops big and small looking for the best deal they could get on whatever their hearts desired. Outdoor restaurants with colorful umbrellas lined the tree-covered streets for those who wanted to sip frozen daiquiris. Slim women in large hats and colorful sarongs hurried along the streets full of bicycles carrying cargo—human and everything else.

CHAPTER 1

Yes, This Is Rangoon

Yes, this is Rangoon. What a town. It usually rains in the early morning and at times in the late afternoon. Not too long either time—just enough to keep the temperature down for a while.

Rumors abound in all forms about the possibility Burma could be overrun by the Japanese if they move on Cambodia and Thailand. That's a possibility, but I don't think right away. And who am I? JB Short. Jake Sizemore and I have been friends and partners for ten years. We're first-class smugglers. Welcome to Rangoon.

It's 11:00 a.m. I stand on the veranda of an elegant apartment overlooking Rangoon Bay. The monsoon season is almost over. The morning rain has left large drops of water that slide down the elephant leaves like pearls racing to a drop-off.

This will be another humid afternoon, but Jake and I are going to the Dragon's Pearl Casino owned by Augustine Hertz. His place has a long mahogany bar with teakwood inlay so highly polished it shines like a stream of red wine. It winds its way past gambling tables that are always crowded all the way to the veranda with glass tables that overlooks the boat dock. There, the view of Rangoon Bay at sunset is unbelievable. If you're still sober that is.

Jake throws his linen jacket over his blue silk shirt and adjusts his Panama hat. We go downstairs and out to our waiting rickshaw.

The rickshaw comes to a smooth stop just off the front steps of the Dragon's Pearl Casino. I slip Big Jo a good tip. He's always been our private driver. He knows more about who and what comes and goes where and when. He always has an ear and an eye out for what's going on around the docks and streets and picks up much more than the British do. He has a memory better than any bird dog I've seen. He's been stand-up guy who's been with us for five years. He's well paid.

Large Chinese dragons with big pearls in their mouths hover over the red carpet entrance to the grandest gambling casino in Rangoon. There you'll find enough food, booze, and games of chance for anyone's appetites.

We slip through the private side door Mr. Hertz allows us to use. We go up the stairs to a private alcove with a small table and three chairs. A sparkling jade-bead curtain offers some privacy. We look over the casino and spot our darling Sunny Moon, a close friend with whom we've had good business dealings. She's sitting at a table in the casino with that business friend of hers she had met at some festival in Cambodia. She's a looker. She's dressed in a tight, red, silk sarong slit up the side and silver hair down to the North Fork of the Brazos River. That's in Texas, near Lubbock, where Jake and I had met up in a flight school. That seems a lifetime away now.

Sunny Moon starts to the stairs with the tanned, silver-haired lady who moves like a southern breeze. Jake motions to a private table on the veranda. Seems the silver-haired lady's name is Jada Soon. She has a diesel-powered sampan and a diesel-powered junk with a good, loyal crew, and she's been doing some business along the coast. She always arrives in a high-powered speedboat with one crewman armed to take care of the boat when it's tied up at the Dragon's Pearl dock.

At the private table, Sunny Moon tells us she's been in contact with someone who wants to move some high-grade stuff—jade, pearls, a small amount of gold, and some old family jewels—out of Cambodia before the Japanese overrun the place. Jake and I have three large, well-armed diesel-powered junks she needs for transport.

Jake tells her our boats are out doing some business for Augustine Hertz and wouldn't be back for a couple days. That was almost true. I knew Jake was stalling until he could find out more about Jada Soon.

Who is this silver breeze who just blew in from who knows where? Who's she dealing with? What's the payoff? He and I had the same questions. No one works for nothing on the coast of the Andaman Sea. We'll have Big Jo check her out and see which way she blows. Could be a British agent, American OSS, or worse, works for the Japanese. That would be trouble no amount of money could fix. Some deals are too good to be true. And usually are.

The evening continues. The sun sets right on time. Our tall glasses stay full with whatever nectar of the gods we're having. The night wears on.

CHAPTER 2

I Arise in the Late Afternoon

I ARISE IN THE late afternoon. Rangoon's air is humid and hangs on me like a wet silk sheet. There's a slight, cool breeze coming off the Andaman Sea you can feel if you're in the shade.

Jake and Big Jo are down along the docks looking into couple of leads. Seems that Jada Soon blew into town a couple weeks ago wanting to make a smugglers' run with one of our boats. Jake, being the cautious man he is, does no business with people without checking them out first.

This morning, we received a handwritten invitation to a special gathering of people at Augustine Hertz's office at the casino for a crab lunch and drinks. Now we know something is up. Hertz doesn't invite people up to his private office with the large, one-way glass window on a whim. The glass has images of large, deep-blue waves breaking on the coast on a moonlit night on the casino side, but from the office, I heard you can see the whole casino—the gambling tables and the bar. We also heard that Sunny Moon, Big Jo, and Jada Soon were also invited. This makes Jake a little nervous, cautious.

Sunny Moon is on her way to the meeting. She's just left a meeting at the Japanese diplomatic consul. Her card says she's an investment counselor. She's smiling confidently as if she's just learned where a stone-cold case of long neck beer is hidden. She's a real piece of work. She also often has meeting with the British diplomatic consul at her private table at the Dragon's Pearl dining room. She says it's good for her travel business.

The rumors are that her story starts when she was young. She was sold to a Chinese businessman who took a liking to her. She received a very good education, and she's a wiz with numbers. She also learned all the tricks and scams of running a gambling house, an opium den, a street club, dice, poker, all kinds of other card games, and how to figure odds on games of chance. She learned all about smuggling, how to make profitable deals, and how to put pressure on and how to back it up. At this point in her life, everyone knows Sunny as Chen Loo, Iron Lady. She's making the Chinese businessman a bundle as he enjoys himself with very young girls.

The only problem is that the mistress of the Chinese businessman got wind that he was fooling around with her. The mistress was very pissed off thinking that people were talking behind her back and she was losing face. So she faced the Chinese guy down one night. She berated him and demanded it was Chen Loo or her.

The guy took a long drag off his opium pipe and said, "Chen Loo makes me a lot of money. If you want to do that, you can start as a streetwalker and sell your pitiful body at one of my street clubs. Or you can stay here, keep this house, and keep your flapping lips on your loud mouth shut. Leave me alone. You make me weary."

The next morning, they found him with his throat cut, his lips stapled to his tongue. His balls were attached to bamboo shoots that stuck out five inches from his ears. The rest of that part of him was found stuck right up his old brown eye, his Hershey hole as some people call that orifice.

The mistress was a woman with a bad case of the red ass. Now that she was going to run the business, she was after anyone who had crossed her, and Chen Loo was at the top of her list.

Chen Loo got word about the night's activities from the maid she had put into the home a year before. She wasted no time. She cleaned out her safe, grabbed anything else she could carry, and hauled ass to

Cambodia. It's said she worked at a bank on the coast and set up a small gambling club on the side that she made very successful.

Then word reached her that the old mistress had had her tracked down and was on her way to settle the old score. It gets a little unclear at this point. What's known is the mistress was found in her custom rickshaw upside down in the community septic pool with a sharpened end of a bamboo shaft right through her middle and metal needles in both ears. A long, sharp, bamboo pole had been stuck right up her old wazoo, right up the poop chute.

There was an investigation, but Chen Loo was long gone, and with no witnesses and no confirmation of a large man built a little like Big Joe and an unidentified person leaving the area, they just called it a suicide when she ran off the road in her rickshaw. No one knows or cares now anyway.

A couple years ago, she and Big Jo turned up in Rangoon. Jake and I met Sunny and did some small business with her to start with. Then a little bigger stuff. We found her always straight up, a lady of her word when she gave it.

We gave Sunny our help and backing to make things right when she found herself in a hard place with the Fat Man, aka Henry the Leech. Sunny got into the tourist and businessmen's entertainment business with her first class-operation, the Emporium for Tourists, Businessmen, and Travelers.

Sunny had all-gold rickshaws, and all her men wore red silk coveralls that were cool and easy to wear. She was very tough when it came to selecting her employees, but she paid them well. She taught them to move with their heads up and smiling, and she made them shower twice a day in the rest area she provided. She even selected cologne they would wear. She knew the value of first impressions in her business. She had learned the hard way. It's good business to look good, smile, smell good, and keep your eyes and ears open and your mouth shut. She'd pay her drivers well for any information that proved useful, but the understanding, the rule, was that it was for her ears only, no one else's. Her drivers knew their way around. They were everywhere all the time.

Jake and I had formed the Sampan Transfer Company in 1936 and later added what became a small but very profitable line of diesel-powered junks that were well armed. We call them boats. It was an investment that paid off big in just three months. We called ourselves the China Sea Traders. Some call us the China Sea Raiders, but not to our faces. We don't take kindly to bad-mannered people.

Jake and Big Jo pull up in our rickshaw. Jake seems to be satisfied with the information they dug up. He'd found a very reliable source; a ship's captain who had just come in from Thailand he knew and had done some business with Jada Soon. He put in some good words about her.

It also seems Augustine Hertz had been asking around with just about the same questions we had. He was always very thorough, and you didn't want to make an enemy of Mr. Hertz.

Sunny Moon's driver stops right at the red carpet leading up to the doorway of the Dragon's Pearl Casino. She leaves the rickshaw with a slow, velvety move. She's wearing a tight, yellow sarong with a ruby-red sash around her twenty-eight-inch waist and a large, plum-colored silk flowing scarf covering a wide-brimmed scarlet hat pulled down to cover the top of her dark glasses.

Jake and I move from the alcove and notice Sunny is moving toward the dock bar. We saw Jada Soon has her speedboat tied to the dock with her man watching over things. The two ladies see each other and wave laughing. Hugs are in order for both of them.

Jada sees Jake and me coming down the stairs to the dock and waves us over. Sunny turns and starts to walk toward Jada in a glorious, luscious, graceful way I can't do justice to with mere words. But once you see it, you'll always remember it. I did notice beads of sweat on the back of Jake's neck like just after a hard day's work or those you see on a cold, long neck beer. We stumble down the stairs like a couple of dock lizards. "Hello, ladies!"

I take Jada Soon to the dock bar and order whatever she's drinking and a cold long neck for me. Jake and Sunny are arm in arm strolling and in quiet conversation. They order drinks too, and when we finish them, we start up the stairs to lunch. No one knows what it's all about, but we're on time.

We head up the polished stairway where two large, elegantly finished gold dragons with pearls in their mouths stand beside beautifully carved mahogany and teak doors. The room is an extension of Augustine's lifestyle; everything is highly polished wood and pearl. Dark-blue silk drapes gently move to the breeze off the bay but still keep the room slightly dim. The large, one-way window with the sea scenes on the other side offers a full view of the casino below. Seven plush leather and carved wood chairs are in a crescent around a large, smoked-glass table held up by short ivory legs in the center. The bar, a long, horseshoe affair with polished wood, wraps all the way around between two silk-draped doors at each end and a large smoked mirror. Behind the bar is Big Jo wiping glasses with a smile as if he'd just eaten all our lunches.

From around the curtain at the end of the bar comes the man himself. Augustine gives handshakes and hugs all around. Augie is about five seven. He's stocky but muscular in a way, and he's impeccably dressed from his shiny alligator shoes and black silk dress pants and matching belt to his elegant, maroon silk shirt with dragon-pearl cufflinks and matching rings one on each hand. He's always on time and hates it when the invitation states the time you're expected and you're late. That really ticks him off.

"Thank you all for coming and being on time and in good spirits. First, lunch and drinks. Then we can do what we do best, make a profit. Let us now dine." He claps his hands. Three waiters appear with solid-silver trays bearing the largest crabs and lobsters I've seen in a great while. They're steaming and fresh. Following are three more waiters with first-class champagne chilled perfectly and served in silver goblets with pearl rims.

We finish devouring the crab and lobster and are sitting around sipping champagne, laughing, and passing time with small talk when through the curtain at the end of the bar a large bulk of a man comes in. He's sweating and wiping his hand and double chin with a large engraved cotton handkerchief that looks like a bar towel. His smile reveals two gold teeth. His grunt of a laugh makes him sound like a wild boar looking for his trough. He waddles to such an extent that you think he's about to tip over at any time. Just the kind who sits next to you on a crowded bus.

A cold tension, a bad feeling descends on the room. It's the Fat Man, Henry the Leech, and he's always armed. Some have said he hides a .32 automatic in one of his wrinkles. I don't know if that's true or not. I watch Jake slip his hand under his coat. I knew he was limbering up his ruby-handled .45 automatic. Sunny almost chokes and spits her champagne back into her sliver goblet. Jada grips her cup so tightly I think the champagne is going to pop right out of the cup. Big Jo has stopped smiling. I don't know what he has in his hand that's covered with a large bar towel.

The tension is leading to the desperation you'd feel if you fell overboard and someone threw you an anchor. This is white-knuckle time for everyone. I swear I heard a mouse fart at the other end of the room. The tension gets so high so quickly you could hear teeth grinding. Maybe mine. I slowly move my hand to the small of my back and grip the pearl handle of my .45. I'm waiting to cover Jake's play. If anyone moves to scratch where it itches, it's going get noisy really quick.

As always, Augie laughs. "Let's all calm down. I was the one who invited Henry here today to discuss our differences and come to a profitable business agreement for all concerned. After that is done, you can go outside and shoot each other, okay? Some of you know him as the Fat Man or Henry the Leech. Those names are a crude injustice. For this meeting, I prefer Henry, all right? Fine then.

"I thought he might be of assistance in whatever project we choose to do. With his contacts, knowledge, and experience, he would be acceptable as well as useful. We will air our disagreements and have trust among ourselves. We must all be honest if we want to succeed. Jada, what say you?"

Jada's thinking, *I wonder who puts his shoes on and how long it's been since he seen his toes.* She speaks. "I have dealt with Henry from time to time, and every time, I come out on the short end of the deal. That's happened just once too often. He may have some contacts I wouldn't know. It never worked for me. My cut was always smaller than what he gave his word on. So for me, the price is too high. I have learned the hard way that if it squirms like fat leech, lies and cheats like a fat leech, then it is what it is. I want no part of it. I will leave now if you wish me to."

"No," says Augie. "That won't be necessary."

Fat Henry leaves the bar against which he was leaning and waddles toward an empty chair. He reaches into his pocket. Those in the casino below must have heard the guns cocking. Henry laughs and pulls out a new handkerchief. He reaches the leather chair and lowers his bulk into it. The chair squeaks and groans. Jada laughs and wonders again who puts his shoes on.

Augustine says, "We will never get things worked out with name calling and bickering between ourselves. Let us reach a profitable, mutual accommodation."

"It's not going to be that easy. There's been too much trust gone down the river," Jake says. He leans back in his chair, arms crossed.

Henry squirms in his chair and reaches for another hand towel to wipe his face and hands. Again the sounds of cocking hammers fill the room. Henry says with a grunting sound, "Sizemore, you're crazy if you think you can scare me off this deal. You're just a pussy anyway."

"Be very careful, Fat Man. Don't let your fat face overload your lard ass or your luck just might run out today," replies Jake.

"Ladies and gentleman, please! Enough of this unprofitable talk. It accomplishes nothing and leads to no profit. Nothing good will come of it," replies Augie in disgust.

"Sorry about that, Augie," says Jake. "I apologize to you for my outburst of tension, but still I have to say I'm not going to risk my crew or my boats to someone I can't trust. It's too big a risk no matter what the payoff is. With Henry, the cost is just too high."

"And just what is the cost of doing business with you garbage cans these days?" asks Henry.

Jake, still with his hand under his coat, leans forward as if to rise when Augie intercedes. "What have you to offer, Sunny Moon?"

Sunny has a cold gaze in her eyes. She rises, one hand holding her large hat in front of her and the other hand under it. "I won't do business with anyone I can't trust. I wouldn't give Henry the sweat off a dead dog's balls if he were dying of thirst in the middle of the desert. You have cheated me for the last time, lardass."

"You all are just jealous of my success and the contacts I have. You would cheat me or worse if I ever turned my back on you. As for you, Sunny Moon, you child of a whore, you skinny, slut-faced bitch, shut your face before I shut it for you."

Jake's hand starts out of his jacket, but before he can make his move, Sunny shouts, "That cuts it, you fat ball of shit." The hand she had in her hat comes out with an ivory-handled .38. She puts one in Henry's chin and another right between where his eyebrows should have been. Henry's .45 automatic falls from under his jacket and out of his hand to the floor.

Big Jo and I grab some bar towels and wrap them around his head real tight so as not to get any blood or brains on Augie's good leather chair.

"Ah shit! What the hell! Everybody has a damn gun," Augie says. He calmly walks to the phone and calls his casino floor manager to bring six big guys from the kitchen with six tablecloths to take out some garbage and bring some sandwiches and bring up some cold champagne.

And beer! I think.

"I will leave you all for a short time to handle some unforeseen challenges, but I will return shortly," Augie says.

The smell of gunpowder hangs in the air when the six large men with six large tablecloths arrive to cover the Fat Man quite nicely and haul him off. Waiters appear with a good-smelling fragrance to rid the room of the smell of gunpowder. More waiters come with cold champagne, sandwiches, and long neck beer, thank goodness.

Some mill around the window and gaze at the casino floor while others sip champagne or eat sandwiches or do both. The time goes by like a lead weight tied to your ankle.

Augie reappears in white-linen suit pants with a yellow pullover silk shirt. "Thank you all for being so patient. Seems the problem was more weighty than I first thought. Well, we have drunk and eaten and are in much better spirits. Henry's problem has been solved. Let us all agree to do business in a trustworthy manner. We all agree to agree to this, don't we?"

We all nod in agreement.

"Good. Let's get down to do what we do well, making a profit."

Everyone sits in the leather chairs around the smoked-glass table. Henry's chair has been taken away. Sunny produces maps, charts, a timetable, and a short list of things that will be needed in this business venture. She starts to explain. "A couple of weeks ago, Jada ran into an old friend, she knew as a banking investments man from the Netherlands. As they talked, his conversation turned to whether she knew anyone who could help him move some jewels to Rangoon in about two weeks out of Bancock Bay. No, she told him, but she would check around when she got back to Rangoon. He should call her in a week, she told him. He agreed.

"Jada had the man checked out by a diamond dealer she knew who had contacts in the banking business, and he is who he said he was. She'd done some small stuff with him before and had found him to be a tightwad. That made her feel maybe he was not always honest as he seemed. But he wants this load real bad.

"When she talked to him today, he sounded like he was sweating and needed to move quickly. The trip will require Jake's and JB's boats with extra fuel. Their boats are well armed and can handle the waters of the Andaman Sea. His people will handle the loading under the supervision of Captain Mike and JB.

"We'll need to load as quickly as we can. These are not friendly waters as we all know. If we run into trouble, stay together. We will move into the shallows of the reef islands and try to catch the fog banks. Above all, stay together. We will leave at six, at dusk, so we will look like any other boats that leave for early morning fishing.

"Now the answer to the question you have all been waiting for, what's the payoff." Sunny turns to Augie. "About three hundred thousand or more split evenly."

There is a sound of relief and agreement from the rest of partners around the table.

Jake says, "Before this goes any further, I want it understood and agreed upon that the cost of my boats and trained crews, fuel, and other supplies will be two thousand American for each boat."

"That's a little stiff, Jake," says Sunny, "but I can live with it."

Augie replies, "The money will be at the dock when we shove off. You have my word on it, Jake."

"Then it's done and okay by all of us," says Jada.

Everyone nods.

"Good. Then we will all meet and be ready to go at six. Be at the China Sea Traders docks then. The boats will be fueled, armed, and ready to go. Be on time ready to leave or you'll be standing on the dock and out of the deal. Is that understood by all of you?"

They all say yes. Augie says, "Good. Very good."

CHAPTER 3

So at Six O'Clock …

S O AT SIX o'clock, both boats are loaded and pulling away from the docks. All are aboard with their personal protection, mostly automatics pistols. The evening mist covers their boats like a gray blanket. The docks of Rangoon are quiet this December evening in 1939.

The misty, foggy air is moving off the Andaman Sea pushed by a mild breeze. Captain Mile of Jake's boat knows the waters along the coast—Tavoy Coast, Andaman Sea, and Mergui Archipelago to the Bancock Bay in the Gulf of Thailand. He's been doing these waters for forty years and has been Jake's captain for fifteen years.

The boats cruise easy and cut the water like a knife. They will arrive at Victoria Point in a few hours. Jake and Sunny go below to a large cabin with rugs, leather chairs, and dark-red silk drapes over the portholes. Jake opens the portholes, and a fresh ocean breeze fills the cabin. Jake removes his jacket and shirt and puts them on hangers. Jake is six two and weighs about two hundred. He's well built. His body scars show past dealings with bad-mannered people.

Sunny removes her fog coat, scarf, and shoes. Jake asks, "You want a drink? Booze, beer, or a Coke, or something like maybe green tea cool?"

"Yes," she says. "Put some vermouth over the top."

"I think I'll have a little Southern Comfort," Jake says.

"Okay," says Sunny. She laughs and removes her top to reveal a well-proportioned figure and smooth, slightly dark skin covered by her silky, dark hair hanging down just past her twenty-six-inch waist and blue silk trousers. They sit on the edge of the bunk on dark silk sheets sipping their drinks and making small talk. Sunny runs a soft palm across Jake's chest. "Why have we never made love except in a frenzy of haste?"

"Because we were always too busy thinking about making money."

"Always profit! Not focused on us!"

"That's true."

"It was always food, fun, a frolic, and then back to business."

"Maybe we should have done it differently?" Jake asks.

"What are your plans if the Japanese take Rangoon? Have you and JB got something going?"

"Not really. We were thinking we might hook up with Augie on something big and then pull out before it's too late and things get too hot."

Sunny closes her eyes. "Would you take all your boats if you pulled out?"

"Probably not. If we run all the way to Australia, that would be too far and too rough on the boats. Our days in Rangoon are numbered. It's just a matter of time before Australia will be a buildup area for troops to train to take on the Japanese. I figure the Americans and the British will pour supplies and men into it for a war, and where there's a war, there's men with money who need stuff to spend it on."

Jake looks at Sunny's dark hair and strokes it. "What do you have planned, darling?"

"I might have something going, but nothing I can depend on right now."

She rests her head on his shoulder. She feels the cool ocean breeze coming in through the porthole. Jake turns her head up to look into her eyes. "Sunny, there's always room for you on my boat if that's all right with you of course."

She holds his face in her hands. "I thought you'd never ask." She pulls his head to hers, and they kiss. She puts their glasses on the table. They settle down in the large bunk together. Her back is pressed against his chest. He can feel her heart beat almost to the rhythm of the waves against the boat. His arm goes around her shoulder. She caresses his hand. The sound of restful breathing fills the cabin.

Later, there's a knock on the cabin door. "Captain Jake sir, I think you should come on deck. Two powerboats about ten thousand yards off the aft starboard coming our direction very quickly."

Jake grabs his shirt and flight jacket. Sunny slips into her deck shoes and blouse and grabs a camouflage jacket and binoculars on the table. She heads up to the deck. She and Jake stand by the starboard rail looking through the binoculars at the boats moving toward them at high speed.

"Mike, get some firepower up her quick to repel boarders. Move the twenty millimeter into position to do the most damage with the first few rounds."

"Consider it done," Captain Mike replies. "Just like the good old days, aye, Captain Jake?"

JB's voice is heard over the radio. "Hey, hoss, you want to bring them in real close then have both boats make a quick ninety degree turn. And take them head-on."

"Sounds good, JB. We'll go to starboard for more room to move around. Train your twenty millimeter on the waterline of the second boat."

"Roger that, old hoss," replies JB.

Augie starts yelling, "No! Wait! Stop! There's no profit in getting shot. Bloodshed is almost always bad business. Let me negotiate with them. Let's see who they are and make a deal. There's no profit getting our boats shot up. We can't turn back now. And one boat is not enough for this deal."

"Okay, Augie, we'll play it your way for now, but the first sign of bad manners in any way, I'm not waiting around to get JB's and my crews and people onboard including my ass and your ass shot off."

"Can you tell who they are?" Augie yells.

"No, but I can tell you who they aren't. It's not Popeye the sailor or the tooth fairy."

"They're the Fat Man's boats," Captain Mike says. "I know them well. We've had problems with them before. Unfortunately, they lost both times. A waste of good men. They stayed away from us after that."

"BJ, Mike says those are the Fat Man's boats. I guess they have a new captain now."

"Roger that. I can guess what they want to know. I'll idle down with you and cover Augie's play."

"Mike says the boats are about five thousand yards off and closing."

"Listen," Augie says, "If I can't deal with these guys and it's not going to work out, I'll put my hands in my pockets like this." He shows Jake. "And immediately you can deal with them your way. Some people can't grasp the idea of doing trustworthy business. They don't have what it takes to do good business and make a profit no matter how good you can make it sound."

They can see the gunboats clearly. A crew is at the rail armed with rifles and pistols. Jake and JB have idled their boats down and are prepared to move to a battle position.

On the rail of one of the Fat Man's boat is a dark-skinned Chinese man they assume to be the new captain. As they come alongside at an angle, Jake and JB want them to see their guns and cannons that can be brought to bear on their decks, but they want to keep their hatches closed till the time they're needed.

Augie has come over the rail of JB's boat to Jake's and walks to the rail of Jake's boat just as Mike eases up the cabin stairs and slips a Thompson chopper into Jake's hand from behind.

Augustine Hertz recognizes the Chinese crewman and the man at rail as Chinn Li, the Fat Man's former second in command and now the captain and boss. They had met over the years at different times with Fat Man. The Fat Man had always treated Chinn Li badly and had cheated him several times, but he had stayed loyal because he was well paid at times. But there was never any love lost between them, and neither would turn his back on the other.

That's the reason that why when they left each other, they both walked backward until they were out of knife and even gun range. The story goes that when Mr. Li set up a small opium smuggling operation out of Cambodia, the Fat Man took a percentage but then got greedy and kept squeezing Chinn Li. When it was more than he could stand, Chinn Li went to his supplier and killed him and his whole providers and runners in a gruesome manner just so the Fat Man couldn't take over the rest of his operation. He didn't. There was no love lost between those two.

Augustine says to Chinn Li, "Come alongside, my friend. What brings you to the coastal water of the Andaman Sea?"

Chinn Li replies, "Captain Hertz, a gentleman told me of your departure from Rangoon docks. Poor man. He should have told me before you left. He would be having breakfast with his children this very morning with gold coin in his pockets, but instead, his body is food for the fishes. But this is not why I wasted so much good fuel to catch up to you. It has come to my ears about the Fat Man. I want to know why you had him killed!"

Augustine looks dismayed, depressed, sad. "Say it is not so that you would think so low of me to do such a dreadful thing. No, Chinn Li, my friend, it was not I who brought the end to your friend's days."

Augustine clasps his hands as if in prayer while Chinn Li stands with one foot on his rail, smiling between a set of green rotting teeth with two gold ones up front. "I was with him oh, just yesterday. We were discussing an opportunity that was to be profitable for all involved, but he was not happy evenly sharing or working with others and got carried away and departed. No, I did not have anything to do with his departure, though I can understand your concern. But in truthful remorse, there were times when the thought of sending him to his ancestors crossed my mind."

Chinn Li moves to the rail of his boat to face Augustine across the water between them. "I think that is the biggest pile of water buffalo shit or bilge off the back of a Rangoon garbage boat that I have heard lately. But I am not unhappy that we can lie to each other and both know it as gentlemen and friends sometimes do. We both know Henry was a lying piece of fresh elephant crap, a leech of the first order. He told me about this deal we were going to do with you and that if it went his way, he would share seven percent with me, but he was lying of course. But three percent is better than being tied to the dock in Rangoon!

"But the bottom line is we never got paid, and someone is going to pay that loss of income even if the Fat Man went to his ancestors before they were ready for him to waddle in."

"This we both agree on, about his being a unsavory person and dishonest. We both lost money on the departure of Henry," says Augie.

Chinn Li says, "Oh yes, but I ask myself where you would be going in the dark of night with empty boats across the dangerous waters of the Andaman Sea chancing bad weather and with men with unsavory reputations as Jake Sizemore and JB Short."

"Yes, well, times are changing, and in the course of doing business, we can find ourselves with questionable associates. I am sure you have the same problem from time to time."

Chinn Li laughs to the extent he shows a row of rotting teeth with the two gold ones in the middle. You could almost see his bad breath. "I must confess that I had plans to do that leech in if things did not improve. He was dealing with the Japanese at different times. They cheated him, then he cheated me. I hate those slant-eyed bastards. They kill everyone! But if you don't tell me where you're going, I will kill you all and burn your boats or take them for myself. So what do you say, Mr. Hertz?"

"Well, I say I expected more out of you than to throw away six percent of a deal and kill too." Augustine turns and smiles at Jake.

"I could take everything—all the cargo—and then kill you. What's this about six percent?" Chinn Li asks.

"That was to be the Fat Man's cut," Augie says, "but if we don't go through with it, we will all lose money. There is no profit for anyone in that. We have no cargo onboard at this time."

"I will travel to this place and protect you from coastal bandits," says Chinn Li.

"No." says Augie. "This deal is contracted for just two boats. Any more than that will scare the deal off for fear of a trap. Then we will all lose."

Chinn Li walks up and down the deck rubbing his jaw with one hand and scratching his leg with the other. "You think I'm just going to wait here while you go off to do good business and then cheat me out my six percent? You have been reading too many fortune cookies, Mr. Hertz."

Augustine holds his chin in his right hand and his elbow in his left hand, eyes closed, as if listening intently to Chinn Li. "Mr. Li, it is so distressing for me that you so willingly throw away a large profit over an emotional moment that none of us can change. But we can turn a bad situation into a profit for all concerned. And why would you think we would come into these waters unarmed? In trying to force your way onto our boats, you would lose half your crew and maybe a complete boat and would be worse off and on top of that make no profit. Look, Chinn Li, we all know that in the very near future, we will end up at the mercy of a foreign interest that wants to destroy us all. Now is the time for us to pull together and put aside old differences to do good business for a profit while we still can.

"Mr. Li, I have never given my word and not kept it. It's a matter of honor. I am sure the same is true with you. Let us do good business with trust and honor as gentlemen who will mutually profit. There will be no crying in the morning of widows and orphans. You will have put coins in their pockets, and you will be held in high esteem as the best man on the China Coast. What say you to profit, Mr. Li?"

Augustine smiles his best, most confident smile and then slips one hand in his pocket. Jake is as stone-faced as I have ever seen. All hell will break loose on Chinn Li's boat if Augie's other hand moves to his pocket.

Chinn Li replies, "You say what you think I want to hear. You sound like a crowing chicken just before it is thrown into the pot. But what you say is true. Give your word that the six percent that was the Fat Man's cut will come to me. Is that the agreement?" Chinn Li puts his foot on the rail with his shoulders thrown back and another rotten-teeth smile on his scrawny face.

"Absolutely. We are in agreement then as gentlemen," Mr. Hertz says. "Wait here two days. We will return low in the water, and you can escort us back to Rangoon to split the cargo. Good trading!"

Chinn Li says, "But don't think we can't find you should you be delayed."

"We will see you in two days, Mr. Li. Stay safe."

Jake yells to Mike and JB, "Wind it up and stick them in the wind."
They move away swiftly, their bows rising out of the water.
Li watches the boats get smaller very quickly. *Augustine Hertz must think I'm a stupid fool if he thinks I'm going to stay here two days. I will wait till their boats are out of sight then move up past Victoria Point. If they make their turn around the bay point loaded with cargo, they will be sitting ducks. I will kill them all, take their cargo, and sink their boats. As Hertz's body floats by, I will ask him who he thinks the fool is now.*

CHAPTER 4

The Boats Ride High in the Water

THE BOATS RIDE high in the water under the power of the twin engines. Jake brings Augustine's favorite drink—a double cognac—and a long neck for himself. "Great work, Augie. For a while, I thought he was going to slip off the hook. But you know that rotten- mouthed weasel is lying through his rotten teeth and can't be trusted. He'll wait till we start back when we're heavy and low in the water. He'll want to catch us when we're turning the bay point, loaded and not as fast. We may be able to outgun him at short range and do more damage than he wants to handle. I know for a fact he doesn't have any twenty millimeters. The Fat Man would never buy them. Too much weight, too expensive. He has most likely three or four fifty calibers. A few rifles was all I saw, and a few pistols, but them fifty cals can still do a lot damage and damn sure kill you," says Jake.

Augustine looks at Jake and pats his shoulder. "Right, but I still have a card to play."

"Hope it's an ace," says Jake.

Everyone comes up from belowdecks for some fresh air and to ease their tension. Augie says, "Let's all fill our glasses and toast to a quick loading and safe trip to Rangoon."

All the crew and everyone else raise their glasses and cheer.

The boats pass Victoria Point. Jake and Sunny are sitting on the deck with their backs against the bulkhead and their feet resting on the railing. The clouds almost cover the moonlight, but the smell of the open sea is refreshing. It's quiet except for the throbbing of the engines that move the boat swiftly across the Andaman Sea.

"There's Victoria Point. A nice place to settle down and have a nice, quiet life." Jake leans back as if he's engaging in some wishful thinking.

Sunny smiles. "I can't see you feeding the ducks, bird watching, walking the reef looking for seashells."

"Well, darling, nothing lasts forever. What future would Sunny Moon have for herself?" asks Jake with a smile as if he already knows the answer.

"I don't know for sure, but something always comes up even if the sun doesn't." She laughs. "And what would the great Jake Sizemore, raider known up and down the China Coast, think I should do?" She slides her hand under his coat and pulls herself around to face Jake.

"You sure you want an answer right now?"

"Yes, right now."

"You want to hook up with a China Coast raider during these unstable times and conditions, not knowing what lies ahead, and put your money on a slow horse? It's not like you to make a bet like that."

"I'm not betting on a slow horse, and in our business, tomorrow is never guaranteed. I am committing everything I have including my heart and soul on a winner, a first-rate, stand-up smuggler, a winner, first at the finish of a long race to the end."

Jake pushes back her long, black hair and stares right into her eyes. He whispers, "I might be in love for the last time."

Sunny caresses his cheek. "And I'm in love for the first time."

Jake pulls her close. Their bodies come together as one in a long, embracing kiss—tender and smooth but with intense desire.

The voice of Augustine Hertz comes from the forward deck. "There's Bancock Bay and a slow fog bank rolling in behind us. Things couldn't get better."

In the distance in the mist is a small speck of a light they assume is the dock. JB and Jada come up from the cabin of their boat arm in arm, looking to see the dock and if anyone is on it. The speck is getting bigger. JB says across the water in a low tone, "This could be a Japanese trap. We're sitting ducks here."

"Bring your boat just ahead of mine so you can cover the whole far end of the dock with your twin twenty millimeters. The first sign of bad manners turn them loose on that end of the dock then power your boat up and do a ninety degree back down the bay. I'll cover your ass from behind, but wait till I wave before you start shooting."

"Okay, hoss, but be careful. These are sneaky bastards."

The boats idle slowly to the dock. A crew member jumps out and secures the boat for a quick exit. The time passes like turtle pulling an anchor. Everyone's starting to get nervous gun hands. The crew on the dock is armed with fifty caliber Thompsons, and Jake's twin twenty millimeters are looking right at the dock and able to cover halfway down. All on deck have Thompsons also.

Jada tells JB, "Don't worry. He is a very cautious guy. He just wants to make sure who we are." She pulls a small flashlight from her jacket and blinks it three times. At the end of the dock, a light blinks twice. A man starts out of the bushes at the end of the dock. He is walking very quickly with a small business case in one hand and a hat in the other. Jada and Sunny jump to the dock and walk toward Helmut Schroeder, the Netherlands man.

He waves his hat across his chest. Two men emerge from the bushes, one pushing and one pulling a heavy cart down the dock. The dock groans and squeaks under the weight of the cart. Schroeder is wearing a white linen suit with a black silk shirt, white tie, and white leather shoes too large for him, and a white linen hat that looks like something a guy would wear if he were in a 1930s gangster movie. He retrieves some papers from his case and shows them to Sunny and Jada. They speak. They shake hands. He waves for the men with the cart to move faster.

JB and Mike are on the dock armed with Colt .45 automatics.

Helmut says, "Quickly! Please hurry. There are bandits in this area, and maybe a Japanese patrol at times. Be quick. We must hurry!"

The cart rolls to a stop just short of the end of the dock. The two men strain to keep it from rolling any farther. Jake's and JB's crew help with the loading under the watchful eyes of JB and Mike. The loading goes smoothly, quickly. The engines idling for a quick departure are putting a strain on the old dock. The guys with the cart start back up the dock with an empty cart except for a bag like doctors carry sitting in the cart.

Helmut shouts to Jada, "Wait! I have forgotten something. Please stop! Wait! Don't leave me. I'll be just one moment." He turns and runs up the dock to the cart at the end of the dock, grabs the bag, and starts running down the dock to the boats. At the same time, the two cart men drop the handles of the cart. One jumps into the bay, but the water is shallow. He's up to his knees in mud hurrying fast as he can to deeper water. The other guy runs into the bush.

Six men jump out of what appears to be a 1930 Buick four-door sedan screaming, "Stop, you bastard! Stop! Helmut, you lying son of a bitch." Five chase Schroeder down the dock while the sixth stops at where the one cart man is in the mud and puts three shots into his back. He falls forward still stuck in the mud, bent over, facedown. The six guys are almost up to Schroeder, who is running as hard as he has ever run in his life. He looks like a circus clown in his big, floppy shoes, coattails flying behind him. He screams, "Wait! Don't leave yet! Wait!! Don't leave! Help me!!"

"Bullshit," says Jake. He thinks it's a trap. "Mike, wind them up and get those Thompsons up here now!"

Jake waves at JB, and the sound of a twenty millimeter machine gun going off flies across the bay. The Buick disappears in a ball of flame. One of the men in the lead running down the dock screams, "Schroeder, you son of a whore asshole, you'll never cheat a Bancock Bay man again." He put four rounds right between his shoulder blades with a Luger. Helmut falls to the dock face first. The little black bag flies out of his hand, hits the dock, and rolls to within three yards of Jake's boat. Jada jumps the rail of JB's boat to the deck of Jake's boat. In two strides, she's on the dock, sprints to the little black, grabs it, and turns around. The five men are running after her. "Stop, bitch!" says the first man. He raises his gun.

JB screams, "Run baby, run! Duck, damn it! You're in the line of fire. Jump, baby!" She leaps and lands just inside the rail of Jake's boat and rolls across the deck. All hell breaks loose. It sounds like Chicago during the twenties. Jake's trained crew—all four with Thompson choppers—were holding fire till Jada was clear of their line of fire. They spray the whole dock with a solid hail of lead. Augie is standing next to Jake with both .45s blazing away. He stops only to reload. All six men are cut down and killed in short order, but two crewmen go down the dock to make sure there are no witnesses.

"Good work, boys. Don't waste too much ammo on those bastards. They cost thirty-five cents apiece," says Jake.

JB shouts to Jake, "Let's get the hell out of here. The noise and what's left of that Buick will draw a lot of bad-mannered people."

"You're right about that, hoss," says Jake. "Mike, cut the lines. I don't want to pull the dock over. Wind them both up three-quarter power and get us upriver quick."

Both boats rpm up instantly, make ninety-degree turns, and move side by side into the cover of the mist and fog. They move like silent ghost images of boats in the late night and early morning in Bancock Bay.

"That was an unpleasant event I had not planned on and almost got out of hand," Augie says. "And that poor son of a bitch Schroeder turned out to be nothing but a greedy bastard who got his ass shot off for a damn black bag. I don't care how much was in it, it's not worth getting your ass shot off. He was just a damn thief, and not a very good one at that. He should have stayed with what he knew. Which obviously was not much, the poor prick." Augie is cleaning and reloading all his clips for his .45s.

"It won't be too long till we get to the point and around into the Andaman Sea," says Jake.

"Don't be in any rush," Augie says. "Jake, take it slow. I don't want to get to the point before eleven a.m."

"Okay," says Jake, "but that's going to make us late getting into Rangoon."

"Better late and alive in Rangoon than floating dead in the Andaman Sea."

Jake comes down to where Augie is sitting in a wicker chair finishing his cleaning job. Jake has in hand Augie's favorite drink, a double shot of cognac, and a long neck beer for himself. "You know I never mess in your business at any time, but considering the cargo, the crew, and our lives, don't you think you should let me in on just what the hell is going on?"

"You're absolutely right my, friend," Augie says. "So here it is. A couple of weeks ago, a Japanese embassy man I know casually came to me with some information I thought would be useful. It seems the Japanese had stepped up their patrols of the China coast all the way past Victoria Point with the idea of destroying all shipping that might be helping the British or the Americans and Chinese, including any smugglers' boats they could find, as they plan to take it over when Rangoon falls.

"These patrols are heavily armed with five-inch deck guns. They come upriver every other day, and this morning, it's their day to run the river. I thought if we could delay our arrival time at the point to turn upriver, they just might run into Chinn Li, who would be waiting in the shallows to savagely attack us. He'll have no way to maneuver without running aground. The two gunboats of the patrol could easily handle Chinn Li and take care of him for us. We should be able to hear the gunfire across the peninsula. And a light fog bank off the Andaman Sea wouldn't hurt us either. So there you have it, Jake. What do you think?"

"That's one hell of a plan. One mistake by anyone, them or us, and we most likely wind up facedown in the Andaman Sea or the richest and luckiest bastards on the coast, so let us make it work and be damn lucky and rich!" answers Jake.

The boats continue on in the mist of the early morning. Augie has gone below. Jake is on deck in a wicker chair with a long, skinny cigar between his fingers. He is leaning against the bulkhead and his boot is on the rail. The hum of the engines is all you can hear. Jake thinks, *That was a close as it gets. Too damn close last night. I wonder how long that kind of luck can last. At some point, your number comes up! I don't think I'm going to continue this way much longer. The strain's too great.* He figures the deals, the action, the excitement, the thrill of not dying one more time, those things aren't fun anymore. He admits things have changed. Every trip, the risks get greater. The boats could be shot to hell and so could they.

The boat expense, all the payoffs, and most of the good repair guys have pulled out already. The fuel cost is fifty-one cents and rising. When you can find it you have to buy all you can get and store it before it stops coming in.

He remembers the close calls JB and he had had, like the time they were jumped by Thai bandits just off the coast. That was a hell of a day. Their boat had taken heavy damage, and they lost three good men. They had left the bandits with one boat sunk and the other so badly damaged the crew had to swim to shore.

Jake considers the worst was when they ran the blockade across the Bay of Bengal. The Japanese almost put more holes in us than it could stand. JB had been hit a couple of times trying to save one of the crew. That had scared the shit out of Jake; he thought he'd lost JB, but luckily, the shots went clean through and he survived, but it took them a month to get the boats back in shape.

They had had some tough times, but they had made big profits and had a good life. But with the political problems, people wanting a bigger payoffs, the generals and the diplomats with their hands out for more knowing the Japanese are going to overrun the British then steal everything. He was afraid there would be nothing left of the once great Rangoon. *Everyone who stays will end up in an internment camp. And the time might be shorter than we think. I'm not going to wait. I'll tell JB. He might want to stay a while, but I doubt it. Will Sunny really leave Rangoon to go with me? I don't know what she'll do.* He hopes to hook up one more deal with Augie to make enough to leave by March.

CHAPTER 5

The Boats Are almost to the Point

THE BOATS ARE almost to the point. "Go slower and listen for gunfire across the peninsula," says Augie.

Everyone on both boats come to the railing and listens intently. JB and Jada are on the deck, her with the little black bag. JB says, "Darling, I'll never figure out just what was going on in that sweet head of yours when you jumped over the decks of two boats onto a dock that was under gunfire just to get a little black bag. Baby, you could have gotten shot up or worse, killed. I tell you I never saw anything this side of hell that even came close to that stunt. What the hell were you thinking?"

Jada smiles and loops her arm in his. She gives him a loving, thankful squeeze. "I thought that if that guy was going to risk his life, his everything to retrieve that bag, it must be worth a lot, so I grabbed it. But if I find a chicken sandwich, some noodles, and a fortune cookie in here, I'll be so pissed I'll go back and shoot him again."

"Let's open it and find out if I have to turn around so you can shoot him again," says Jake.

Jada opens the bag slowly and shines her flashlight in to make sure there were no snakes in it for protection. She puts on a canvas glove just in case and reaches into the bag, revealing more jewels than she could hold—pearl necklaces, inlaid gold with pearls, rubies the size of sparrows' eggs, solid-silver bracelets inset with small rubies, and coins, silver and gold minted in half-pound coins. Jada pulls out a jeweler's loupe and inspects some pieces. "This is the best stuff I've ever seen. Top grade. These jewels must have be cut by Tibetan monks way up there somewhere. I'm telling you this shit is the true family jewels. Never been anything like this seen on the China coast anywhere. Only just a very few jewelers in the world has ever stuff this good. We'll have good bargaining power when we start to fence this. No telling how high the bidding could go, maybe as high as three hundred thousand or more. What do you say now, JB Short?"

"On to Rangoon and let the bidding begin."

"Listen," Jada says. "Gunfire."

Everyone can hear the noise of cannon fire. Judging by the time between the shots, it's about nine to ten miles away, maybe more. They also hear heavy machine-gun fire. Both boats reduce their rpms. They hear more cannon fire and explosions. The gunfire subsides. It's quiet again. The boats slowly move around the point into the fog. All the crew are at the bows of their boats watching the water's surface for the coral reef. The boats are lower in the water now, and the coral could easily put holes in the hulls. They're also on the lookout for any wreckage or bad-mannered people hanging around.

After a few moments of this, they are alarmed and astonished by the sounds of large boats with big engines coming toward them through the fog. As they get louder, they seem to be heading south, downriver, toward the Andaman Sea islands. The wakes of the boats reach Jake's and JB's boats and push them toward the reef, but Captain Mike and JB increase their rpms and get back on course.

One of the crew shouts, "Wreckage ahead." They pull out some long poles on the deck and push some wooden wreckage away from the boats, which are moving slowly. Wooden crates, empty oil cans, clothes, bedding, pots, wood with large holes in it. A body floats by, no arms, facedown. Then two more with enough lead in them that it's a wonder they still float. They see more bodies bobbing in the water. A body with no head but wearing a boot on the left foot similar to those Mr. Li wore. A small rope tied around the torso was connected at the other end to Mr. Li's braided hair pulling his head to and fro with his face up. His two gold teeth had been removed it seemed by a large knife. Whoever had taken them had left all his green and yellow teeth. His head had been severed very cleanly as if by a sword. One of his eyeballs is hanging out of its socket and moving around in the water where his nose used to be. The fish were having their breakfast already.

Some of the people are pleasantly leaning over the side rail puking. The fog begins to lift. They see half of Chinn Li's boat shot to hell but still sticking out of the water. No one speaks for a while. Jake yells, "Okay Mike, JB, wind them up. Let's get the hell to Rangoon before any bad-mannered people show up looking for us. Who knows what Chinn Li told those bastards about us."

The boats roar to life and rise out of the water as if they're glad to be going home.

Later, Sunny goes down to Jake's cabin. She knocks lightly on the door before opening it. She sees Jake's clothes on the floor by the shower. She can see his body through the shower door leaning with both arms extended above the shower head. The warm water runs over his head, down his back, to his ankles. A small stool sits in the corner with a fragrance of scented soap and washcloth. Sunny says, "Hey Sizemore, how's the shower?"

"Hits the spot. There's room for two if you're willing."

Sunny, now wearing nothing but a T-shirt, pulls that off, opens the door, and steps in under the water. She puts her arms around his neck. He puts his hands on her wet hair and pulls her lips to his. Moving his arms to her waist, they come together.

They seem as one body almost. He lifts her up, and her legs encircle his waist. He lowers her and consumes her wetness as sounds of passion increase. Her nails are leaving marks on his shoulders. Her teeth are marking his neck. She sits on the stool, her legs still around his waist. His hands are on her firm butt spreading her cheeks to increase the depth of his probing. She pulls his hands up to her nipples that are so hard they could punch holes in a cardboard box. His mouth covers them, and that brings them to a high moment of desire, passion, love, and relief.

They lean back under the shower grasping each other. They wash each other with the scented fragrance. Jake bends down, taking her in his arms. He pushes the shower door open with one foot. She turns the shower off with her free hand. He takes her to the large bunk and gently lays her down and gets in beside her. They rest in each other's arms, exhausted.

CHAPTER 6

We Reach Rangoon

We reach Rangoon. We don't go to the commercial dock but to the dock under the Dragon's Pearl, where there are large doors at both ends of the dock well hidden with an exit to the street. The doors open and reveal an area large enough for three boats. Stairs lead from the dock to Augie's private office entrance.

Everyone helps unload the cargo, making sure none of it gets misplaced. We ascend to the private office. Augustine orders champagne and excuses himself. The rest of us tell the waiters what we want to eat and drink. We gather around the smoked-glass table with the ivory legs. We're all worse for wear but are in a happy mood. I mean, none of us got shot or killed, and we'll all drink to that.

Augustine comes into the room dressed in blue silk dress pants and a blue pullover silk shirt smelling of a fresh shower, powder, and cologne and wearing his usual good-natured smile. "Thank you for still being here. As friends and business partners, let me congratulate you all on your successful completion of a very hazardous and dangerous business venture that I must say was full of a few unexpected events. But we all survived, I'm happy to say.

"As you all know, we are faced with a foreign invader that to my most up-to-date information is at this moment on the march to Burma and expected to be in Rangoon by March thirteenth. These are not people who can be dealt with in a profitable business manner. As Jake might say, 'They are very bad-mannered people who just get worse.'

"I tell you I don't intend to spend any part of my life in a Japanese internment camp. Therefore, I am planning to leave Rangoon shortly. If you wish to stay in Rangoon and take your chances, I say good-bye and best of luck to you."

A shocked silence falls over the room. Jada downs her champagne and goes to the bar. Big Jo pours her a double whiskey. I think I must have missed something or hadn't heard him right. I look over at Jake. He has a surprised look of *What the hell's going on here?*

Sunny sips her champagne as she looks at Augustine.

"Don't you think the British army can hold them off?" Jada asks.

"No, never," Augie says. "They have no air support from the Americans and aren't going to get any from England. They are strictly going to fall into a defensive position they can't hold considering the Japs control the air and can bomb at will. Those who plan to stay in Rangoon and deal with the Japs have my sincere condolences. I wish them the best of luck, but I wouldn't count on it. Those of you who will be leaving, I will have your cut of our last business for you tomorrow morning, but please after eleven o'clock."

Everyone is wondering what the hell just happened. Augie looks around the room and laughs. "Good. Very good. Let's all raise our glasses to our profitable venture and new profitable ventures elsewhere."

Fresh champagne comes in with crab salad and a fruit plate. There is a sigh of relief throughout the room. We enjoy all that is served. After a short time, we gather around the smoked-glass table with the ivory legs.

Augie says, "Several months ago, Sunny Moon came to me with a very intriguing proposition. For some months, she has been grooming a Japanese diplomatic consul who has an office at the Bank of Rangoon and handles accounts in the vault of the bank for the Japanese. It seems this gentleman is simply fascinated with very young girls. His wife and bosses no nothing about this or even the house he has for his pleasure. He also loves to gamble, and he has an opium habit.

"Sunny suggested I let him win at the tables, and after he believes he can't lose, I let him run up a tab at the tables. When he's so far over his head, we would show him an easy way to not only clear his debts but also acquire more money than he could spend in a lifetime. By putting the pressure on, we get the vault information and rob the Bank of Rangoon before the Japanese arrive and can do that themselves."

There's stunned silence in the room. Doubts begin to come up.

"How in the hell will we move it?" Jake asks. "It would take a lot of two-ton trucks to move that amount of cargo. Are you planning to take everything in the vaults? I mean paper money, trust deeds, safe deposit boxes, gold bars, coins, everything? That would take all day. I don't think they'll just stand around while we take their stuff, and they damn sure aren't going help us."

"We have made arrangements to handle that. We will do it at night," Augie says. "We will take only the gold bars, coins, jewels, and everything in the safety deposit boxes. Except for US dollars and British pounds, money won't be worth the paper it's printed on. We will get all the needed travel and use permits and trucks from a certain Jap general whom we have led to believe will profit from this venture with more riches than Solomon and a certain British lieutenant in the army supply office who thinks he's helping nuns get young women out of Rangoon before the war starts. He is also a frequent patron of the Temple of Pleasure, owned by Sunny Moon, something he would not like to be known widely. He is in the bag already but of course knows nothing about the bank venture we're planning.

"The Japanese, on the other hand, even though they know nothing of the plan, are murdering scum of the worst kind. As they realize what's happening, they will want to ride along to protect their investment and kill us. However, they will be dealt with extreme care before we sail. The plan will be for JB and Big Jo to see that everything I have listed of the Dragon's Pearl equipment will be loaded into the trucks at my private dock on the night of March fifth. The Dragon's Pearl will close on March third and fourth for some electrical repairs and broken water pipe problems.

"The trucks will leave the dock below the way they came in, out thru the doors that lead to the street, at one thirty a.m. and drive across the Sittwe River bridge to the Irrawaddy docks, where the boats will be waiting. The information we are receiving from our Japanese diplomat so far has been first class. I checked it out myself. Any questions?" Augie asks.

"Yes," says Jake. "How are we supposed to get all the cargo on the three other trucks and around the guards?"

"I do admit that was a problem," says Augie, "but with the help of the very greedy diplomat, we were able get three of our men to be among the guard detail of six who are usually on duty. They will have fresh, unopened champagne from my bar. The champagne will be loaded with a tasteless but extremely effective soporific that will not wear off for twelve to fourteen hours."

"Why not just kill them and be done with it?" asks JB.

"Because I don't want bloodshed or loud noise, and we need someone to take the fall for looting the bank. They will be prime suspects. It should throw the Japs off for at least five to six hours. The guard change is at eleven p.m. Our men will be in place by eleven thirty. The three trucks will park one behind the other, and one of our people will stay with the trucks to make it look official. Everything must be loaded by two a.m. and at the docks by three fifteen. Boats will leave no later than five fifteen. Any other questions?" asks Augie.

Jada asks, "Will Sunny and I go with JB on the first set of trucks that leave at one thirty from the casino or wait with Jake and Big Jo?"

"The ladies will leave on the casino's trucks, and ladies, please, come prepared to defend yourselves if it becomes necessary. As we have found out on our last outing, sometimes, things don't always go as planned. I might suggest you wear slacks with deck shoes or leather shoes—no high heels or slip-ons that might slip off."

Augie walks to the bar and picks up some papers. He hands one to each of them; they contain schedules, route of travel, boat loading and departing times, time at the bank, and arrival at the dock.

"When are we going to handle the unwanted passengers?" asks Jake.

"They will be sent away as soon as the bank trucks arrive. They will join the river lilies before we leave. If there is any unforeseen trouble, stay together. I don't expect any until the bank truck arrives. Understand this. Make no mistake. We are dealing with the devil's toilet bowl of people, true septic tank dwellers, and if there's going to be trouble, I believe it will come before we unload the bank truck. They will not want to reload the trucks again. We will prepare for as many possible misadventures as we can.

"The general and the diplomat will arrive at the docks in the general's staff car around two thirty a.m. I suggest everyone arm himself or herself with extra clips and ammo. It might come in handy. But I believe everything will go as planned, so let's fill our glasses high and toast to this profitable venture. The Bank of Rangoon!" Augie shouts.

The others respond in kind. From this point on, there's no backing out. The champagne flows freely. Augie is talking with Big Jo. He waves Jake and JB over and tells them, "Just in case some bad-mannered people show up, I want a clear sign that something is wrong before we get in too deep. When you pull in, put the truck spotlights on me along with your bright lights. If something's wrong, I'll give you a wave with my hat to come on in. If I put my hands in my pockets, slow down and arm yourselves well. Stop short of the dock. Then turn your truck lights on high beam and direct your spotlights on the general and the diplomat to blind them. Kill them both and anyone they may have hidden or brought in," says Augie.

"We have week to prepare so let's get to it," Jake says.

The week passes slowly. Everyone is getting things in order and preparing to leave Rangoon. Sunny Moon set in motion the plan she had to sell her Emporium for Tourists, Businessmen, and Travelers to an Austrian investment company working out of the Bank of India. To not raise any questions, she tells everyone involved she's traveling to Hong Kong. She gets agreements that the people running the business will stay on with no change in the operation. A company made up of British officers bought the Temple of Pleasure for some reason. She transfers all her funds and assets to the Port Moresby Bank of Australia.

Jake and JB make sure all their boats are in top running condition with extra fuel barrels and plenty of ammo. They sell all the sampans to Captain Mike for fifty dollars as a present for his faithful service. Jake tells him to hang low till after the war is over and he will become a rich man with the tourist trade. Jada sells her sampan and boats to the captain of her crew. She also wires her funds to Sidney's Bank of Australia. Augie signs over his casino to his casino manager and trusted right-hand man, Poe Ling, for a nice sum of gold. It will be his on the seventh of March.

CHAPTER 7

The Sun Dips into Rangoon Bay

THE SUN DIPS into Rangoon Bay. Jada Soon and JB Short are having a few drinks on the veranda of the Dragon's Pearl for the last time.

"You know, Jada, this will be our last sunset in Rangoon. Why don't we watch it from my apartment balcony? It's not far from here. I'll get a couple of bottles of champagne and two glasses. We can be there in five minutes."

Jada grabs him by the hand. "Let's go before we miss it."

Out the casino doors they go. Big Jo's rickshaw carries them away.

Standing on the balcony, leaning on the brass rail, Jada and JB watch the orange globe cast a golden glow on the bay. A cool breeze sweeps in from the bay. The sunset makes the horizon look as though it's on fire.

"What a view," Jada says.

"Nothing like it anywhere in the world, but having you here to share it with makes it so much better," JB says.

"My, JB, you're a true romantic at heart after all. I just now realized that." Jada puts her arm around his neck while holding his hand at the small of her back. The reflection of the fleeting sunset off the water changes her silver hair to golden.

"We could make it truly memorable you know, if you would be interested," JB says.

"What took you so long? I thought you would never ask." She moves his hand from the small of her back to her firm butt as they walk inside. The silk curtains wave in the breeze.

As they move toward the bedroom where two large bamboo fans keep the silk-sheeted bed cool, they leave a trail of clothes even a blind raccoon could follow. They reach the bed. Their naked bodies come together in a lusty embrace. JB slips a silk pillow under her hips to increase her pleasure. With her arms around his neck, she gives him a long, deep kiss. He slips through her tanned thighs. They both make sounds of pleasure as they slowly explore each other's body from several angles and in every crevice.

Sometime later, in exhaustion, they release each other. Their wet bodies rest next to each other. JB leans over to the container holding the chilled champagne and fills two glasses. They raise their glasses to each other and sip the champagne while smiling lovers' smiles as they look into each other's eyes.

It's 10:00 p.m. Everyone is in his or her place. The cargo has been checked and doubled checked. At 11:00 p.m., the truck arrives at the bank. The lieutenant unloads the new guards, and the old guards climb into the truck. The lieutenant hurries them along as fast as he can. The officer and the old guards pull away.

After a few minutes, Big Jo pulls out a bottle of champagne. "Free drinks for all!" He gives a big laugh and pours the three guards large drinks in their metal army cups while the other two guards stand out front. The guards drink up and laugh. Then they fall over. The doctored drinks have worked faster than expected.

The three guards are quickly propped up in the windows to give the appearance of guarding while the three trucks pull up outside the bank one behind the other. The loading begins. Jake puts the key into the first security gate's lock, but it doesn't turn. He struggles with it for a few moments. Big Jo wants to know what's wrong. Jake tells him the key doesn't work. Big Jo wants to try it. Jake says, "Don't break it off in the lock, damn it."

Big Jo rushes away and returns with a half-full bottle of champagne. He shakes it hard and points it at the keyhole. He removes his thumb. The fluid gushes though the keyhole to the other side of the gate. A large, drunk cockroach staggers out of the keyhole and drops over, its legs wiggling. They try the key again. The lock pops open. "It just needed a drink," says Big Jo.

The combination for the vault supplied by the Japanese diplomat works like a charm. It takes two men to manage the larger boxes. The two guys in the other trucks help. They easily handle the bags marked with US dollar and British pound signs, but the jewels, gold coins, bracelets, and other jewelry from the deposit boxes takes longer to get in the bank bags. Big Jo handles the boxes of gold bars to see they are loaded evenly between the trucks to prevent overloading. Buy two a.m., they are finished. They leave everything outside the vault just as they had found it, including three guards propped up at the windows.

Sunny Jada and Augie with the three trucks from the Dragon's Pearl have already crossed the Sittwe River bridge and have gotten most of the cargo in the first boat.

"Well, ladies," says Augie, "we are almost ready to set off on a great adventure in the new environment of Australia. I hope you don't mind I took the pleasure of loading a good supply of champagne and cognac onboard. Why leave it to the Japs? They certainly don't deserve it, and one must have some amenities on a long trip. We will raise our glasses and toast a fond farewell to lovely Rangoon."

General Shojiro Tida and Japanese diplomatic consul Surie Takeshi arrive in the general's command car and stop just short of the dock. They exit the car and start toward the three of them. The general salutes, and the diplomat tips his hat with a smile. The general extends his hand to Augustine Hertz. "Congratulations. It appears our endeavors have met with success, and we are almost ready to leave. But I see only one truck?"

"Yes. The first truck has been put on the boat. We await the arrival of the second truck momentarily," says Augie.

"Are these your mistresses?" the general asks.

"No. They are my business partners. I believe you know the lady Miss Sunny Moon, and the other charming lady is Jada Soon."

"Yes, I am familiar with both women. I have files on them as well as other mistresses, whores, wives, and lovers of all I deal with. But doing business with stupid women is no way to do business. My women see to my needs only, as all women should."

"Of course and correctly so," Augie replies. "Here comes the other truck over the bridge."

The general shouts in Japanese. Seven soldiers appear from the trees and tall grass at the edge of the dock clearing armed with rifles. As the trucks approach, the general pulls his pistol and tells Augustine to give the signal to come on in.

Augustine pulls his hands from his pockets and waves his hat. He puts his hands back into his pockets. The truck pulls up with the headlights shining in the faces of the general and the diplomat. The diplomat removes his high hat and wipes the inside and his brow with a handkerchief and says, "Finally, the gold and riches are ours!"

"What do you mean ours, you ignorant, little, scab on a pig's ass?" the general says.

The diplomat stops smiling as he looks into the barrel of the general's pistol. He drops his hat and turns as if to run. A shot is heard. A bullet in his right ear blows away the left side of his head.

Soldiers start to move forward. JB and three of the boat deck hands rise from the last boat near them armed with Thompson .45 caliber machine guns just as Jake, Big Jo, and the driver from the last truck also armed with Thompsons run toward the Jap soldiers who can't see them behind the bright headlights of the truck. They cut down the soldiers in a long burst of gunfire.

The shocked general looks toward the truck with the headlights on and fires. Sunny quickly draws her ivory-handled .38 automatic from her waistband and shouts, "Hey, General Shitface!" She puts a round into his lower jaw and another into his right eye while Jada puts a round into his jaw and another into his left eye. This is just as he is cut in two by machine-gun fire from the boat. Augustine is on one knee with both of his .45s shooting at the soldiers.

As quickly as it started, the battle stops. It's quiet again. No one speaks for a few moments. JB jumps from the rear of the boat and runs to Jada. "Are you hit, babe? Are you okay?"

She smiles. She shakes her head. She grabs her right arm where a bullet had gone clear through. No major damage.

Augustine was hit in the upper thigh, but again, it was a clean shot—no broken bones. Jake is at Sunny's side, holding her and asking if she is okay. "I'm okay. But no bastard calls me a whore. I won't stand for that."

"Don't worry about it. He won't be talking to anyone," says Jake.

The smoke and smell of gunpowder still hang in the air as Augustine with his pant leg torn open and tourniquet around his leg tells everyone to get the truck unloaded before other bad-mannered people show up.

The loading starts immediately. Those needing first aid get it. Little Pete, the driver of the third truck, tells Jake he's going back to Rangoon. He will put the dead bodies in the truck and get rid of them somewhere inland and come back with couple of guerillas. If it's safe, they will take them across the border to India where they can be traded for guns and ammo.

Jake thanks him, shakes his hand, gives him a hug, then pays him in British hundred- pound notes.

Little Pete says, "Good luck, Jake, wherever you're going. It's been one hell of a ride, and I wouldn't want to have gone on it with anyone but you and JB. See you after the war." He leaves to load his truck and slip away.

CHAPTER 8

It's Now Five A.M.

IT'S NOW FIVE a.m. Everything's loaded. The boats are fired up. All who are going are onboard. Darkness still covers the dock, but it will be daylight soon. They pull away from their beautiful Rangoon and look back, each lost for the moment in the memories and the adventures they all had in the good days there.

The boats move smoothly with the heavy cargo. They're making good time. The clouds are hiding the moon. Everyone is belowdecks sitting on crates. Augustine Hertz has enough champagne on each boat, so everyone, including the small crew, would be able to drink to their apparent success in the profitable endeavor. As the boats come alongside each other three abreast, they all gather at the sterns of their boats to raise their glasses of champagne.

The sun burns away the clouds and fog in the Andaman Sea. It's late in the morning, going toward noon. JB comes up on the deck, and as the boats come together, JB jumps across the rail to Jake's boat. He tells Jake, "The shit has hit the fan in Rangoon. I'm getting all kinds of traffic on my radio about the bank job. The three guards were questioned then shot. All traffic has been stopped going and coming out of Rangoon. They're searching all boats on the coast and burning any they suspect of collaboration with the thieves. They know six army trucks are missing. That's the good news. They're sending out scout planes and six high-speed attack boats to cover the Andaman Sea for any boats that left last night without checking with the harbormaster."

"We can't shoot it out with armed gunboats, and we sure as hell can't outrun them," Jake says. "Has anyone seen or spotted anything?"

"No" says JB.

"We need a place to hide. They've radioed ahead already. You can count on that. We're slipping into bad water with bad-mannered people. Shit. We have to get into the tall grass and reeds, but the water there is too shallow for our loaded boats."

Augie, standing at the cabin door and listing to the conversation, addresses Jake. "I was afraid something like this would come up. We're unable to outrun or outfight them, and we can't hold off their aircraft. Jake, pull into Victoria Point to the small dock on the left. The tide is coming in now. It will be deep enough for us. We can cover the boats with some camouflage tarps I acquired from the British supply depot. We'll stay hidden long enough to load the three Junkers 52 trimotors. It will appear from the air like business as usual. Late in the day, we can fly away. Everyone will have to help get the goods onto carts and onto the planes, but it can be done. It will be better that getting shot. I can tell you from personal experience that is unacceptable."

"When the Japs show up, what saves these people from getting shot?" JB asks.

"All they have to do is show order demands and manifests for delivery from a company in India," Augie says. "They do business there as well as with some Japanese diplomatic orders. We tell them India because we want them looking in the opposite direction we're going. We need all the time we can get. Pull into Victoria Point as soon as we can. Let's get started."

In a few moments, Victoria Point comes into view. They position the boats one behind the other at the dock. Everyone helps cover the boats with the camouflage covering. A small tramp steamer rests just in front of the boats so it would look it was being unloaded to the aircraft.

It's very humid and hot. The unloading is taking longer than expected. Then there comes the sound of large patrol boats and seaplanes. Everyone hides except for those handling two carts pulled by oxen. They wave as the planes fly overhead. The pilots dip their wings to get a good look. The pilots wave back and turn to follow the patrol boats heading downriver.

CHAPTER 9

This Is Serious Shit

THIS IS SERIOUS shit. They'll be back in a few hours looking along the shore. We couldn't waste any more time. It takes more heavy lifting by everyone to get the planes loaded. Jada and Sunny help with whatever Dragon's Pearl stuff they can lift. Jada's arm starts to bleed, but one of the helpers applies an herb powder and the bleeding stops. He puts a new bandage around it. He does the same to Augie's wound as he was helping all he could.

The Australian pilots are directing the loading so the planes will be balanced and able to get off the ground. They want to be ready to leave when the wind comes off the bay to give them the lift they need to get airborne. A few cases of champagne and some overstuffed chairs don't make it onto the plane.

After the boats are unloaded, Captain Mike comes over to say good-bye, and we give him and his crew a good number of crisp hundred-pound notes. Of course Captain Mike gets the boats, and the crews will follow him. The boats, very light in the water, will go to Bancock Bay to lie low for a while.

Jake and I got a little teary eyed as we shook hands with Captain Mike. Augie gives him a case of champagne as a good-bye gift. The coverings over the boats are removed. With full fuel tanks, they turn away from the dock. Everyone waves as the boats power up and roar away to Bancock Bay.

Jake and I, hats tilted back on our heads and hands in pockets, watch as they disappear out of Victoria Point. Jada and Sunny put their arms around our waists and watch with us, knowing how we feel.

It's getting late. The expected breeze is coming across the bay. Augie pays the airport crew and the crew of the tramp steamer and gives them three cases of champagne and the overstuffed chairs. The Australian pilots yell, "Wind it up, boys! Let's get the hell out of here while we still can. Time to go or stay!"

We all leave the dock and run to the planes. The planes taxi to the end of the runway and turn into the wind off the bay. There's just enough room in five seats for the passengers. The noise of the three engines is loud and gets louder. We have to cover our ears. It takes all their power and the entire runway for the trimotors to get airborne.

We rise over the Andaman Sea and head up to fifteen thousand feet. As we climb, we can see the Japanese patrol boats and seaplanes in the middle of the sea turning around and heading back to Rangoon.

We fly, all the planes in view of each other. For a while, no one speaks. Augie reaches back for a crate and reveals eight large champagne bottles nestled in straw and ice. Glasses too of course. He explains that the same is on all the planes as he didn't know which one we would be in. Our pilot radios the other planes and tells them they'll find champagne onboard too. We fill our glasses, the pilot too. Augie says, "To a good conclusion of a very profitable endeavor. Even with a few unplanned events, it went well. No one got killed, so onward to a profitable future for us all!"

We toast each other.

Sunny has a grip on Jake's arm. "I've never flown before, but being with you, I'm not afraid."

"We'll never be far enough apart to ever be afraid again," Jake says.

I hold Jada's hand. She grips my arm. "Penny for your thoughts, JB."

"I can't think of my future without you in it." I give her a lover's smile and kiss her forehead.

Jake toasts Augie. "Here's to you, the man who thought of everything."

"Well, not quite everything," says Augie. "I forgot to piss before I got on the plane."

We all roar with laughter as we fly into the sunset to Australia and to profitable new lives. Back then, we weren't contemplating the war. We didn't know it wouldn't end until 1945 and change the whole world in the process, us included.

ACKNOWLEDGMENTS

Judy Cutler, the one who had the faith and encouragement
And a great research assistant and a friend,
who I drank a lot of coffee & tea with late at night.

Maynard and Jaynie Yutzy, the two great people
they never lost faith in me even when I was lost.
Always putting up with me in our travels, never
Failing with encouragement.

And To All The People Who lived
THE BANK OF RANGOON
JB. Short
Jake Sizemore
Sunny Moon
Jada Soon
Augustine Hertzz

Printed in the United States
By Bookmasters